Cock-a-doodle-doo!

For my brother, Neil

Look

Copyright © 2018 by Fiona Woodcock

All rights reserved. Manufactured in China.

For information address HarperCollins Children's Books,

a division of HarperCollins Publishers, 195 Broadway, New York, NY 10007.

www.harpercollinschildrens.com

The artwork and hand-lettered text was created by hand-cut rubber stamps,
stencils, BLO pens, and additional pencil line work, all composited digitally.

Library of Congress Cataloging-in-Publication Data is available.

ISBN 978-0-06-264455-8 (trade ed.)

18 19 20 21 22 SCP 10 9 8 7 6 5 4 3 2 1

First Edition

Greenwillow Books

An Imprint of HarperCollinsPublishers

FIONA WOODCOCK

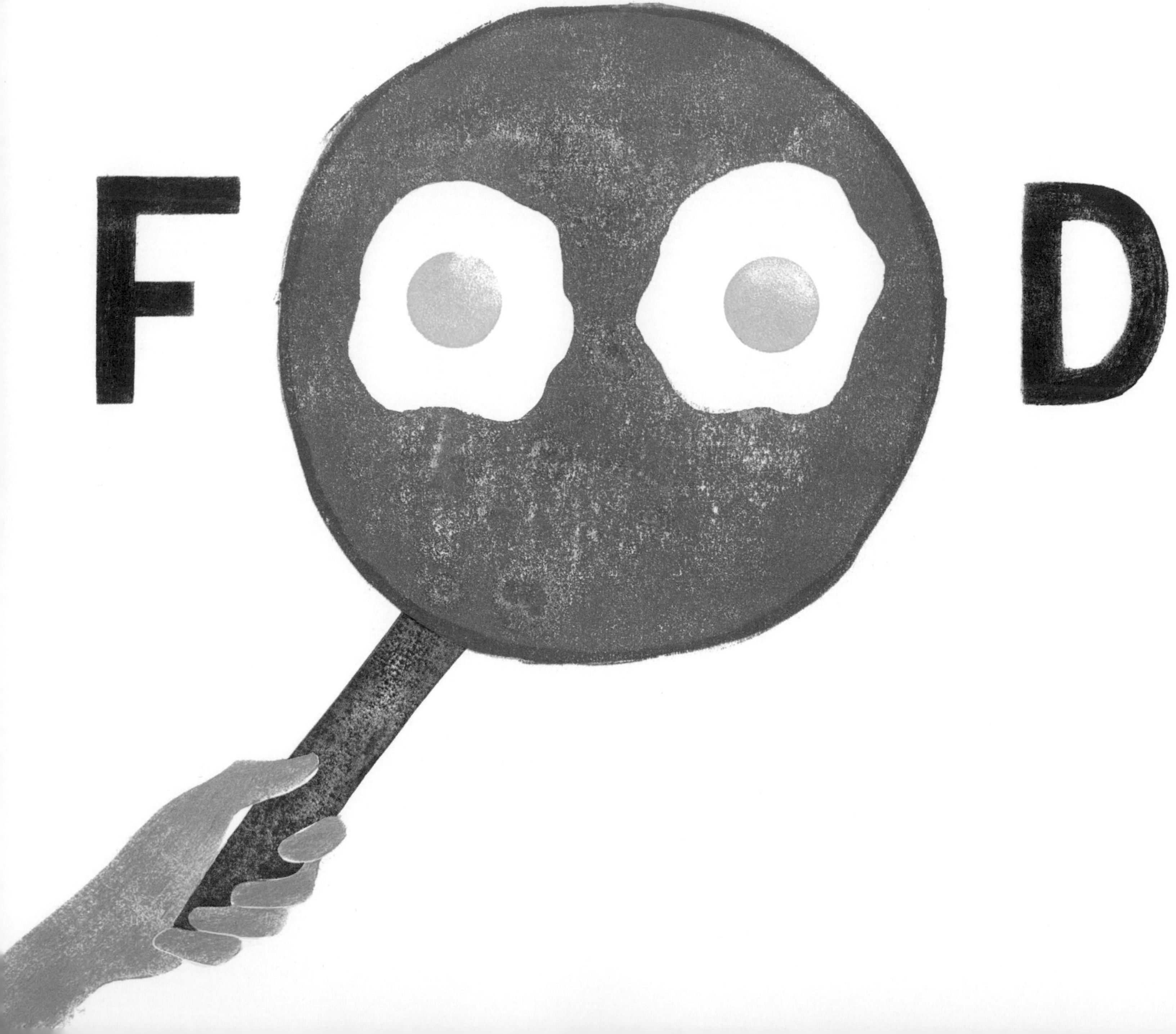
FOOD

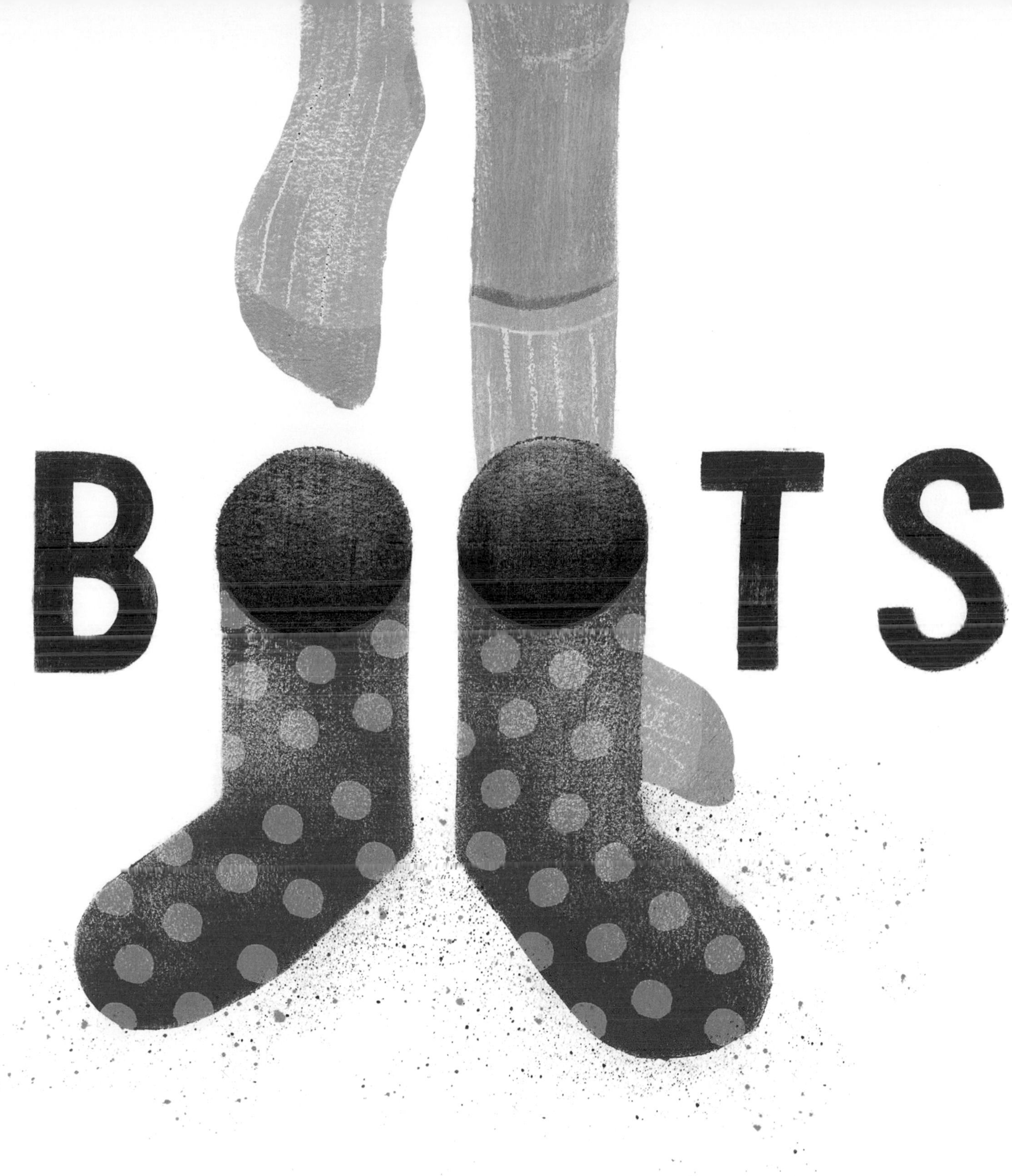
BOOTS

Zoo

hooray!

kangar

cockat o o

BABOON

LOOK

balloons

aCHOO!

WOOF WOOF

OOPS!

(boohoo)

BATH
ROOM

shampoo

snooze

good
night

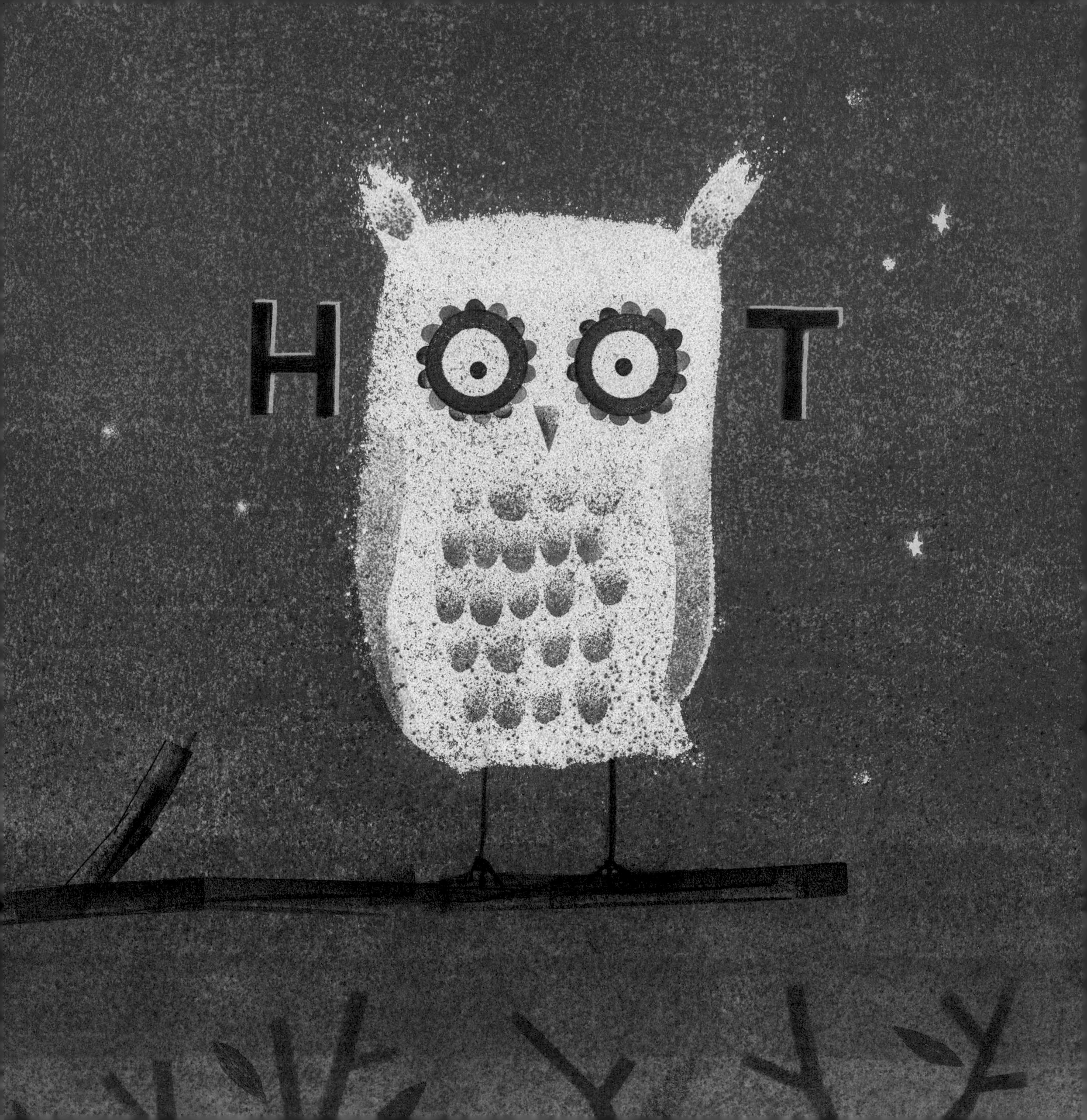
HOOT

moon